Beyond the mind

Leukos

First Published in April 2023

ISBN: 978-93-5741-251-3

BLUEROSE PUBLISHERS

www.bluerosepublishers.com

info@bluerosepublishers.com

+91 8882 898 898

Cover Design:

Yash

Typographic Design:

Hemlata

Distributed by: BlueRose, Amazon, Flipkart

PROLOGUE

This book was written in a state of a real psychosis and trying to make sense - and arriving at certain conclusions. There is some knowledge that is authentic that swoops you off your feet - then, there are the ones that don't.

The agenda of this book are numerous. One of those has been to try to seek a release or try to encapsulate a situation - that would have taken me lifetimes to wrap my head around. Obviously, I couldn't do justice. But you know who could? These guys –

Dolores and Jung, your work has been a great source of wonder, joy and inspiration and a piece of solace in the darkest of times. I hope whoever reads this book is filled with an equal zeal to dwell deeper within themselves and is inspired to open their hearts and minds to find whatever it is that they want to find.

There are no two things in this Universe. There is only the endlessness of now and a cesspool of chaos that is bred out of human thought. Your utmost interest lies in being light-heartedly and fully invested in yourself until you have conceptualized who you are. There is plenty of fun in the process. Almost wouldn't wanna make you draw near the end.

Το λευκός, I hope you've found the treasures and/or the lessons that you dwelled into the shadows to find. Never forget, no experience is lost on you. You have a lot to offer. Find the light within you, as others find it within themselves.

Hic Rhodus, Hic Salta! Do the dance here because there is no turning back.

PREFACE

Not to rip off Van Gough, but when I was a kid, the sight of the sky made me dream too. There could be nothing more beautiful than stars that lit up like jewels in the night sky. It triggered that essence in me that makes you dream of beautiful things - whatever that is to you. My head was filled with all sorts of little ideas of what beauty could be. How there could be nothing more beautiful than Earth looked at from space. So, I would dream about becoming an astronaut.

But as I grew up and my taste developed, as opposed to the heights, I now became more concerned with the depths. A lot of my taste budded from wanting to understand the self and how we can use consciousness to lift the quality of existence. There's plenty of ways you can go about this question. I chose the path of the warrior and thus, began the road to deep inner work. Naturally, I gravitated towards psychology. The conception of this book has been possible as a result of a developing taste that was brought on by a fit to understand some of the events that had transpired in my own life, and in doing so to develop a tribe of people who are interested in exploring the inner world and transforming the outer through it.

Ladies and gentlemen, I beg the question - how deep do we go until we start to soar higher?

TABLE OF CONTENTS

MODEL OF THE PSYCHE

What if your comfort zone is a padded cell and Lucifer in jackboots has affixed 95 of these to the door explaining why you are exactly where you need to be?

The beliefs that fuel a person make up the chamber of their reality. Based on the interaction with the world and yourself, you develop a sense of self. The Earth game and rules thus far have been designed to make you forget any sense of self you might have left after incarnating on this planet. Any easy access to our true self is hidden behind layers of conditioning - what you think of yourself, what your friends/family think of you, what society wants you to be and what cultures expect you to be.

For instance, if you are born and bred in a household which fosters codependency then you will inadvertently find yourself associating comfort with authority and thus leave behind substantial possibilities of finding your own beat to existence outside of this training set.

All these paradigms that others choose for us close us off to our own authentic conception of reality. This is until we are left with a hollow shell of a human who is too scared to explore anything outside of the comfort of this padded cell. But if you do find your authentic self worthy of being saved from this rigid program designed for the human conditions of living and treat your life as a science project then read on.

However, before we get into any of that, we must understand the thing that generates the human conditions of living – the psyche. I won't just make you go on my word for it, but actually prove how reality is very much like a video game and we are a crazy scientist trying to hack into the system. And science requires models!

The following is Jung's model of psyche interpolated over David Oliver's model of the mind.

JUNG'S MODEL OF THE PSYCHE

Jung divides the psyche into the conscious and the unconscious, whereby the conscious comprises the persona and the ego, and the unconscious comprises the personal unconscious and the collective unconscious. Together the conscious and the unconscious make the Self. Now, let's try to comprehend each individual component on its own.

PERSONA

This is a part of the personality which comes into existence for reasons of adaptation according to personal convenience. It is that part which we show to the world. The persona has been called the packaging of the ego, the ego's public relations, and a necessity of everyday life. One might say that one's social success depends on having a reasonably well-functioning persona, which is flexible enough to adapt to different situations, and which is a good reflection of the ego qualities which lie behind it.

THE EGO

Jung saw the ego as the center of the field of consciousness, which contains our conscious awareness of existing and a continuing sense of personal identity. It is the organizer of our thoughts and intuitions, feelings and sensations, and has access to memories which are not repressed. The ego is the bearer of personality and stands at the junction between the inner and outer worlds. A flexible ego means greater perceptibility of the unconscious via the conscious.

THE PERSONAL UNCONSCIOUS

To quote Jung, 'Everything of which I know, but of which I am not at the moment thinking; everything of which I was once conscious but have now forgotten; everything perceived by my senses, but not noted by my conscious mind; everything which, involuntarily and without paying attention to it, I feel, think, remember, want, and do; all the future things which are taking shape in me and will sometime come to consciousness; all this is the content of the unconscious'. 'Besides these we must include all more or less intentional repressions of painful thought and feelings. I call the sum of these contents the "personal unconscious"'.

The personal unconscious is a product of the interaction between the collective unconscious and the development of the individual during life.

THE COLLECTIVE UNCONSCIOUS

The collective unconscious corresponds to that part of the mind containing memories and impulses of which the individual is not aware. It is common to mankind as a whole and originating in the inherited structure of the brain. Jung took the view that the whole personality is present in potential from birth and that personality is not solely a function of the environment, as was thought at the time when he was developing his ideas, but merely brings out what is already there. The role of the environment is to emphasize and develop aspects already within the individual.

Every infant is born with an intact blueprint for life, both physically and mentally, and while these ideas were very controversial at the time, there is much more agreement now that each animal species is uniquely equipped with a repertoire of behaviors adapted to the environment in which it has evolved. The individual inherits these 'innate releasing mechanisms' in its central nervous system which become activated when appropriate stimuli is encountered in the environment.

THE SHADOW

The Shadow is a part of the unconscious, but can at times break into the conscious field. It carries all the things we do not want to know about ourselves or do not like. It often possesses qualities which are opposite from those in the persona, and therefore opposite from those of which we are conscious. Here is the Jungian idea of one aspect of the personality compensating for another - where there is light, there must also be shadow. If the compensatory relationship breaks down, it can result in a shadow personality with little depth and excessive concerns for what other people think about them.

The shadow is a complex in the personal unconscious with its roots in the collective unconscious and is the complex most easily accessible to the conscious mind. The way in which we most immediately experience the shadows is as we project it onto other people, so that we can be fairly sure that traits which we cannot stand in other people really belong to ourselves and that we are trying to disown them. While difficult and painful, it is important that we work at owning our shadow to bring it into relationship with our persona, and so provide greater integration moving towards the self.

<u>**THE SELF**</u>

The Self for Jung comprises the whole of the psyche, including all its potential. It is the organizing genius behind the personality, and is responsible for bringing about the best adjustment in each stage of life that circumstances can allow. Crucially, it has a teleological function: it is forward looking, seeking fulfilment. The goal of the Self is wholeness, and Jung called this search for wholeness the process of individuation, the purpose being to develop the organism's fullest potential.

It is a distinguishing feature of Jungian psychology that the theory is organized from the point of view of the Self, not from that of the ego. The ego, along with other structures, develops out of the Self which exists from the beginning of life. The Self is rooted in biology but also has access to an infinitely wider range of experience, including the whole wealth of the cultural and religious realms, and the depths of which all human beings are capable. It is therefore capable of being projected onto figures or institutions which carry power: God, the sun, kings and queens and so on.

<u>**HOW THE PSYCHE FUNCTIONS**</u>

Jung maintained that the psyche is a self-regulating system (like the body). The psyche strives to maintain a balance between opposing qualities while at the same time actively seeking its own development or what he called individuation.

The Self along with environmental influences shape the direction system which comprises Reason and Will. This decides our experience of thinking, feeling, sensation and intuition. All of this together shapes the unique perception system of an individual that gives them a sense of I-ness.

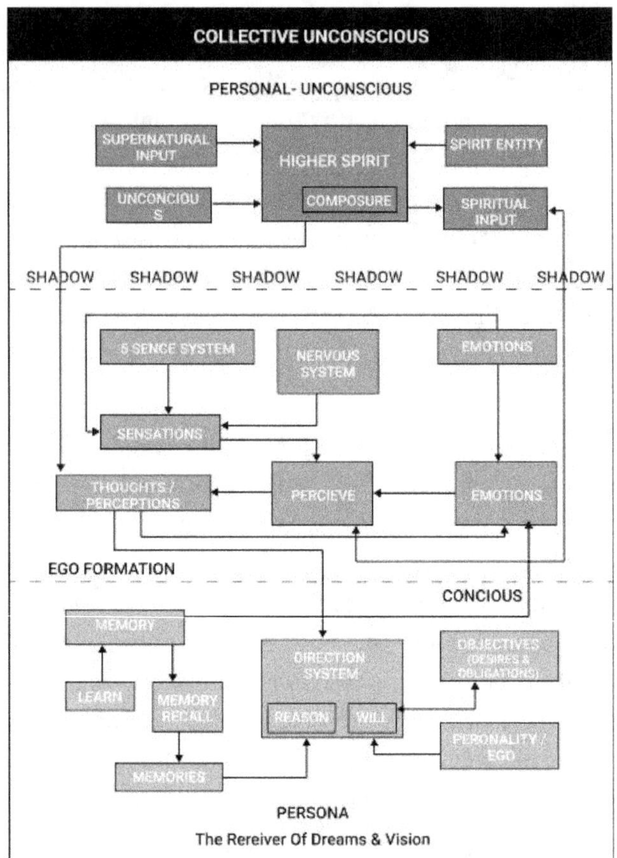

<u>Prompt: Model of the Psyche</u>

This sense of I-ness influences the perception log and shapes and reshapes the way we remember memories, ourselves and others. How we recall memories influences the emotional world which in turn influences the sense of I-ness. In fact, suppressing memories helps us to actually reveal the true perceptions behind it.

Jung noted that people differ in the conscious use they make of four functions which he termed, thinking, feeling, sensation, and intuition. In any individual, one of these functions is superior and is therefore more highly developed than other functions, since greater use is made of it. But each attitude operates in relation to the introversion or extraversion of the person, as well as in conjunction with other less dominant functions.

The way in which people relate to the inner and outer world is determined by their attitude type: an extraverted individual being orientated to the outer world, and an introverted one primarily to the inner world.

PREDEFINED CHARACTER CHOICES[1]

I believe, on some level, an individual can always be playing one of the Jungian archetypes. "These [archetypes] are imprinted and hardwired into our psyches. These are forms or images of a collective nature which occur practically all over the earth as constituents of myths and at the same time, as individual products of the unconscious."

The 12 character archetypes are: The Innocent, Everyman, Hero, Outlaw, Explorer, Creator, Ruler, Magician, Lover, Caregiver, Jester, and Sage.

1. The Innocent - Exhibits happiness, goodness, optimism, safety, romance, and youth.

2. The Everyman - Seeks connections and belonging; is recognized as supportive, faithful and down-to-earth.

3. The Hero - On a mission to make the world a better place, the Hero is courageous, bold, and inspirational.

4. The Rebel - Questions authority and breaks the rules; the Rebel craves rebellion and revolution.

5. The Explorer - Finds inspiration in travel, risk, discovery, and the thrill of new experiences.

6. The Creator - Imaginative, inventive and driven to build things of enduring meaning and value.

7. The Ruler - Creates order from the chaos, the Ruler is typically controlling and stern, yet responsible and organized.

8. The Magician - Wishes to create something special and make dreams a reality, the Magician is seen as visionary and spiritual.

9. The Lover - Creates intimate moments, inspires love, passion, romance and commitment.

10. The Caregiver - Provides care and protection for others in a selfless manner.

11. The Jester - Brings joy to the world through humor, fun, irreverence and often likes to make some mischief.

12. The Sage - Committed to helping the world gain deeper insight and wisdom, the Sage serves as the thoughtful mentor or advisor.

These Archetypes are universal, inborn models of people, behaviors, and personalities that play a role in influencing human behavior.

---

1. The list is not exhaustive.

AN AVATAR WITH AMNESIA

I'm an avatar with amnesia, bound to ideas of humanity, for all this is insanity. The dark ones, they taunt me, while my human mind haunts me.

Dearest λευκός, you'll actualize your idea of heaven on Earth. But in order to feel the fullness of it, you'll forget what you've done. You will then be able to bear the fruits of your creation in its most unbiased and beaming form.

Be careful not to get too attached to an outcome. Wanting something at all costs is never a good sign and is bound to be burdensome. Remember that what your idea of heaven is might not be the same as other people's. So, don't be too eager to make them a part of it. The only constant riding you through infinity is you. So, figure yourself out and see what resonates with your peace. Ideas shift and change over time. But you will be able to do that only once you feel safe in your being, within your energetic system. If something doesn't flow just let it go. Be flexible like water in your conception of reality. Honor yourself. Cry before you reach for self-medication. A good cry is far more healing than a thousand dopamine hits could ever do to suppress the pain. However, if you do drop the ball on staying unattached then remember chaos breeds creation. Be wise in using it as a constructive or a destructive force. Constructive to make something new, and destructive to destroy something old.

UNDERSTANDING THE WEBWAYS OF REALITY

"When you know nothing matters, the Universe is yours... The Universe is basically an animal that grazes on the ordinary, creates infinite idiots just to eat them. And the smart people get a chance to get on top – take reality for a ride. But it'll never stop trying to throw you and eventually it will. There's no other way off."

- Rick Sanchez

According to Yuval Noah Harari, what we think of as reality is nothing but a persistent communal belief. Everything that we know of in the world generates from the human imagination. From 3D objects to ideologies that run the human world, it all finds its genesis in the mind. Most of those hard and fast facts aren't hard or fast at all. They are but figments of the human imagination that will disintegrate as soon as the collective belief shifts.

Donald Hoffman, in his theory of conscious agents, argues that space-time reality itself does not exist anywhere outside of the human mind. He compares human reality to a video game, where the mind acts as the headset.

To quote Hoffman, "Science with all its tremendous successes has only studied the headset. We are just now in the position to start to look at objective reality outside our headset."

We assume that neurons cause consciousness or are identified with consciousness because we see them. But the problem that we have is that we've assumed that there are neurons because we see neurons. But as soon as we bring our vision, i.e., our sensory system into play, we are back in our headset – the brain. Hence, all theories and concepts project back into the space-time user interface.

According to Hoffman's theory, there is no reason to believe that the structure in our perceptions tells us anything about the structures in objective reality. In other words, what we think of as causality in space and time is nothing but a fiction that we all agree upon. Strictly speaking, nothing in space-time has any causal abilities.

In the game of GTA we have a steering wheel and the reason a person can interfere with that steering wheel is because when we turn the steering wheel to the left, we notice as a result the car on the screen turns to the left. And it's perfectly fine when we're playing the game, but it's deeply false. In actuality, the steering wheel does nothing but serve as a useful fiction. Since you're playing the game, just believe it. But if you are a game designer, you would be a fool to think that the steering wheel does anything. You'd have to have a deeper understanding of the software and the hardware of the computer, how you're putting pixels on the screen. And that's what evolution has given us. It has given us pixels that we interpret as neurons. Similarly, for everyday neuroscience it bodes well to believe that neurons have causal power. For instance, the neural activity in such and such sections of the brain helps us perceive the color green. But just like a system designer of a computer game, you have to lose the fiction to write the game, to understand how the game really works.

The 5 senses only give us a manipulated picture of reality suited to our species and life, but the egotistical mind takes the perceptions manufactured by the perception system from the sensory input to be 'real'. The perceptions - if we start to believe they are true - nourish both our beliefs [intellectual] and our negative emotions [affectional], both of which are a big block to progress. Evolution has given us these symbols for survival. A person would naturally believe that matter exists just as it is perceived; and since it is perceived as an image, the mind would make of it, in itself, an image:

"We should astonish him quite as much by telling him that the object is entirely different from that which is perceived in it, that it has neither the color ascribed to it by the eye, nor the resistance found in it by the hand. The colors, the resistance, are, for him, in the object; they are but states of our mind." - Henri Bergson – Matter and Memory

Subjective reality and perception is where delusions and hallucinations stem from. This is what mind-altering substances do – it alters our consciousness to perceive things from a different stance than everyday normal reality. Hallucinations and delusions are, thus, just altered states of perception that do not fit in with the reality perceived by the majority. This is to say that anything and everything can be true at the same time. But for means and purposes of seamless functioning of the society we are taught to be stern in our view of the world. The matter of the fact is that survival, inherently, does not favor true perceptions.

For the seamless functioning of the society we are given standards of what we should and should not like. These come in the form of laws. The human mind is conditioned on every turn. And in this way we learn perceptions.

Perceptions are a sort of log of all our activity. They are a composite view of everything that has happened to us – not just the input from the senses but all the emotions that accompanied the activity - joy, happiness, sadness, panic, fear, laughter, tears, or annoyance. Replaying our Perceptions is in effect like reliving the experience – all of it - from the feelings to the actions.

"Each person is at each moment capable of remembering all that has ever happened to him and of perceiving everything that is happening everywhere in the universe. The function of the brain and nervous system is to protect us from being overwhelmed and confused by this mass of largely useless and irrelevant knowledge, by shutting out most of what we should otherwise perceive or remember at any moment, and leaving only that very small and special selection which is likely to be practically useful." - 'The Doors of Perception', Aldous Huxley, 1963.

According to such a theory, each one of us is potentially Mind at Large. But insofar as we are animals, our business at all costs pertain to the body with its physical and emotional realms. And for means of survival, Mind at Large has to be funneled through the reducing valve of the brain and nervous system. What comes out at the other end is a measly trickle of the kind of consciousness which will help us to stay alive on the surface of this particular planet.

Thus any form of truth is bound to have ingrained levels or projections onto it. Reality is the same hologram that different people experience and project onto differently. Which is to say what's true for me might not be true for you.

PERCEPTION

Perception plays a great role in shaping the individual experience of reality. In order to direct your experience it would bode well to understand how perception works. For instance, if you have an absolutely awful dream, vision or hallucination experience, there is a very high possibility it was constructed from things you have experienced. If you thus watch a large number of unpleasant films, for example, it could be well fed back to you in the form of an equally unpleasant dream or hallucination.

Memory is a structured, classified and filtered version of perceptions. Whereas perceptions are a log of events, memory is more like a structured database. When we learn, we learn perceptions as our basic input.

The perception also acts as a direction system on what to do next. A perception can be a threat, obligation or opportunity that needs acting upon.

Conditioned by the unreal external world, six kinds of phenomena arise in succession when our perceptions manufacture an external world for us; in effect the perception system is a sort of a computer program to turn sensory input into a workable input for living. It in no way represents objective reality. These phenomenons are as follows:-

1. Sensation - The first phenomenon is intelligence/sensation. Being affected by the external world the mind becomes conscious of the difference between the agreeable and the disagreeable.

2. Perceptions and Memory - The second phenomenon is succession/memory. Following intelligence, memory retains the sensations agreeable as well as disagreeable in a continuous succession of subjective state.

3. Desire - The third phenomenon is clinging. Through the retention and succession of sensations agreeable as well as disagreeable, there arises the desire of clinging.

4. Belief systems - The fourth phenomenon is an attachment to names/beliefs. By clinging the mind hypostatized all names thereby giving definitions to all things. This means that we start constructing a separate and subjective reality.

5. Personality and ego - The fifth phenomenon is the performance of deeds. On account of attachment to names, etc., there arise all the variations of deeds, productive of individuality.

6. Action - The sixth phenomenon is the suffering due to the fetter of deeds. Through deeds suffering arises in which the mind finds itself entangled and curtailed of its freedom.

In the individual subjective reality, there is the notion of self, self-awareness and awareness of others. Then, there are experiences of memories, of problem-solving. There are endless experiences. The notion that our experiences inform our action is a notion of free-will. The experiences of free will probabilistically affect the actions.

Everything sifts through the body and mind to give us an experience unique to our minds. It's a good practice to have knowledge of the 12 Universal Laws to better understand our stories and our troubles. It's a step in the direction of mastering our circumstances.

THE 12 UNIVERSAL LAWS

Life is a playground.

In order to play at the game of life, one must be aware of the rules that are rigged in our favor. Understanding the 12 Universal laws make it easier to assign some order to the chaos of the world. It can also bring a person closer to the rhythm of nature. But nature can be terrible as it can be beautiful; it is never steady. It only makes sense to get comfortable with uncertainty. But uncertainty is a little less daunting when there is some order to be found in place.

LAW OF DIVINE ONENESS

It's like that song Echoes by Pink Floyd goes, "I am you, and what I see is me." According to this law, all is one. Every atom in our body, every molecular, organic, and societal arrangement are all intertwined in a more complex arrangement of consciousness, leading all the way up to the collective unconscious. The collective unconscious being the embodiment of unconditional love, teaches us that compassion, quite literally, has the power to change the world. This law already introduces us as a benevolent extension to the Source or unity consciousness.

LAW OF VIBRATIONS

This law states that everything in the world vibrates at a certain frequency. Each soul, each thought, and each entity has a signature vibration. It is the interaction of their ascent and descent that create the circumstances for flow in the outer reality.

For two people to share the same space peacefully, they must share a common vibe. For example, you'll find that people who like to complain will easily find solace and company in those similar to them. The vice versa is also true, in that, as soon as you shift your vibration you'll find certain people and situations seamlessly falling away from your life.

The following two laws are a derivative of this law.

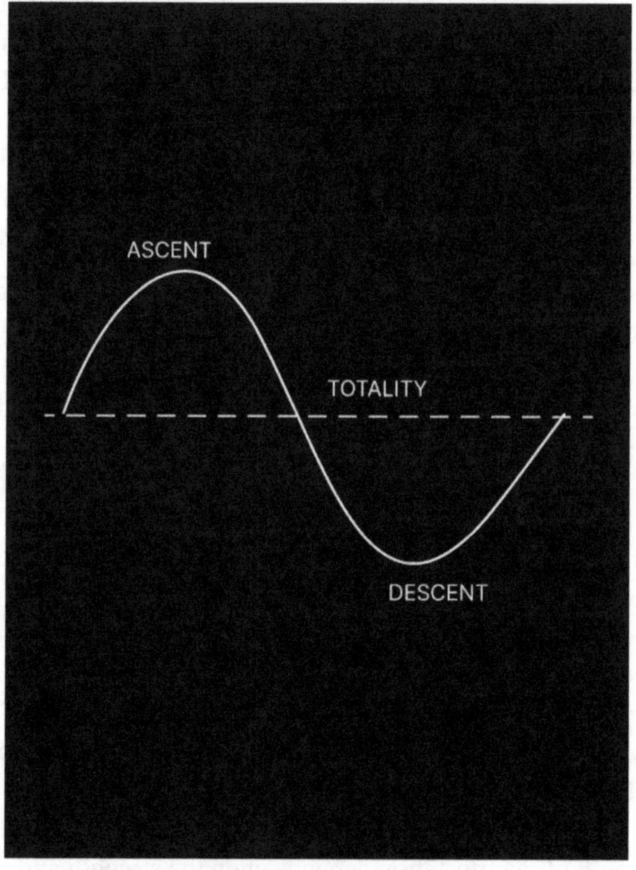

<u>Prompt: The Law of Vibration</u>

LAW OF PERPETUAL TRANSFORMATION OF ENERGY

This law states that everything is in a constant state of flux. The past dissolves in the present and the future stems from the present. The lower vibrations are constantly being transmuted into a higher vibration and the higher vibrations might recycle to ground zero, that is, from the individual human perspective. From the higher perception, everything is always moving towards greater novelty as higher states of consciousness are bound to hold more complexity. The vibrations that have a greater weight tend to assimilate others within it. The weight is decided by the steadfastness within one's own individuality.

As Terrence McKenna once said, "Everything is in the process of fading – your friends, your enemies, your fortunes, your misfortunes…" The only eternal moment is the present moment. In other words, nothing will ever go bad if you don't drop the ball on yourself in the moment of the present experience.

LAW OF ATTRACTION

This law states that like attracts like and is pretty self-explanatory. The Universe only recognizes your vibration. The world is not a reflection of your desires but rather the vibe that you emanate and perceive. For instance, if you are fearful, you attract fearful elements into your reality. This law can be used to manifest circumstances in the outer reality. Circumstances and opportunities are created based on the version of yourself you choose to embody. The strength of manifestation depends upon the strength and will of character that you portray. Figuring out and then focusing on your authentic desires can be used as a safe space for your character in case you start to wonder and get lost within the depths of your own mind.

LAW OF CORRESPONDENCE

This law is summed up by the famous saying, "As within, so without. As above, so below."

This is the tree of the tree and the root of the root in the script of life. According to this law, everything is a pattern which repeats itself. Heaven is a reflection of Hell, and the outer is a reflection of the inner world. The Devil is the shadow of God. And this law is the key to creating utopia on Earth.

If we want to see a beautiful outer world, we must clean the inner world as well. For what we see is a projection of the inner world, manifested outwardly. By seeking this wholeness between inner and outer we can shift the cultural barriers to match higher timelines. To lead a seamless life by striking a balance between the opposing qualities – the shadow and the light – that we all possess.

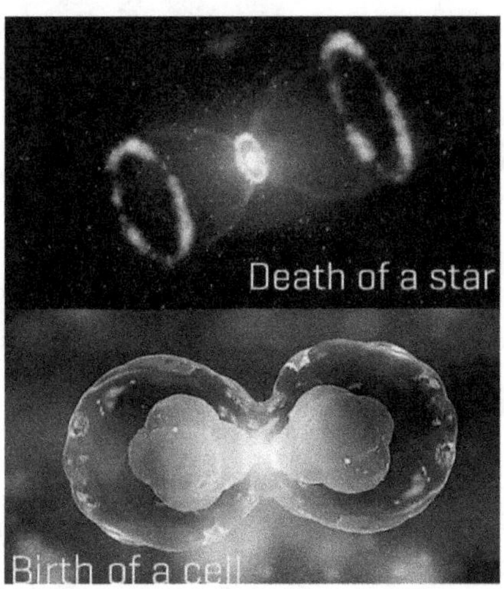

Prompt: Patterns repeat down to the minutest levels

LAW OF CAUSE AND EFFECT

Alternatively known as the Law of Karma, this law states that to every action there will be a balancing reaction. To harness the power of this law, one must take peculiar care in the way they act not only towards themselves but also towards others, because it will affect the balance of the entire matrix. It's like the butterfly effect; the smallest action has a ripple effect through the entire matrix of consciousness. Every thought, every action counts. It's like they say, "do unto others, as you would do unto yourself."

LAW OF COMPENSATION

This law states that you reap what you sow. You are the creator of your reality. For instance, if you put out love, you receive love. This law also puts to test one's awareness of self.

People have a tendency to confuse emotions with intentions. For instance, need in itself points to an inherent lack. So, if you think that these laws can be used as a wishing well, where whatever you think comes true, then you are absolutely correct. It is only a matter of minute discernment and understanding the consequences of your desires.

LAW OF RELATIVITY

Duality is an essential feature to human understanding. We understand day because there is night, yesterday in comparison to today, joy in comparison to pain, and good in comparison to bad. Any event is bound to hold this dual perception. It is entirely at our behest what perception we choose. This also points to the fact that to the Universe there is nothing good or bad. Things just are. Opposing stance is picked at times to sustain the ego.

LAW OF POLARITY

Similar to the Law of Relativity, this law states that everything exists in polar opposites. Experiencing these polarities is part of the human experience, and that they also help us learn from our mistakes and support us in identifying what we don't want, so we can gain clarity surrounding what we do want. For instance, love can take many forms. Because of the multimedia world we live in, we have a tendency to confuse form for emotion. So, when you desire something, be sure if it's the form that you desire or the emotion.

LAW OF RHYTHM

This law states that everything repeats in cycles. The decisions and actions made in between cycles decide whether it is repeated on a lower dimension or a higher dimension. To quote Wilder, "If everything is peachy, then savor the moment, but don't try to make it last beyond the natural order of things. Each stage of life has tremendous gifts to offer." Disaster befalls if a person tries to extend the same cycle for too long. It's best to surrender to the natural state of things. It's like they say, you either go with the flow or are dragged by it.

LAW OF GENDER

This law states that at any given moment a person is operating from their masculine or feminine energy – regardless of the gender they identify with. This can be the shadow or the divine side of masculinity or femininity.

DIVINE FEMININE/MASCULINE BALANCE

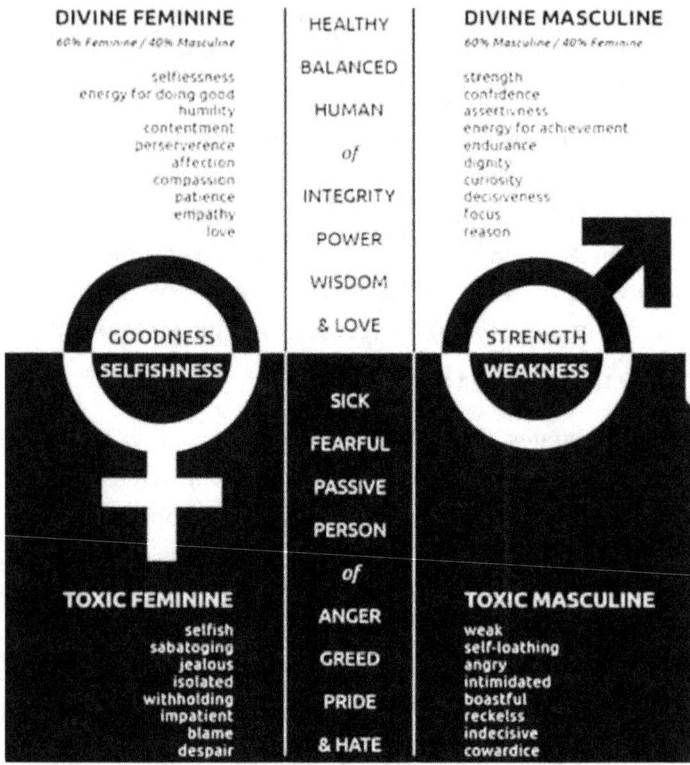

<u>Prompt: Feminine and Masculine Energy</u>

You can use these 12 laws to strategize and fuel the kind of reality you wish to see in the outer world. But remember to keep a balance between forethinking and pleasure. Systematizing thoughts kills reality.

THE PULL BETWEEN REALITIES

"If you're a true believer, if you have some prepackaged philosophy then you're missing out. Because you're prepackaged to ignore what doesn't fit in your model. But if you are septic/witness and then if you push at the edge of the phenomenal world, then the cosmic giggle can get to you."

– Terrence McKenna

The matrix is the default setting to reality. It represents the ways and means of the over-culture and the herd mentality that most find themselves drawn to. It binds the ego to the collective design until an individual forgets everything that makes them – them, and gives an actual soulful experience worth having. So, switch on the telly and relax back. All the blood, gore and glory – there's plenty to tie you down until you've lost all sense of hope, courage, love and salvation.

From the nature of schools to that of democracy, the matrix is ruled by dense elements of fear, loathing, pitting one against another in the name of good governance and competition, and honing duality. Most individuals are so concerned with their outer image that any chance of out-of-the-box thinking, living or having the willpower to explore oneself and one's desires is completely crushed under the pressure of meeting these social standards.

Through being ruled by the distorted masculine energy, the shadow side of masculinity has seeped into the very algorithm of living. That one bit by Bo Burnham has become all too real – [on Earth] life is about three things: getting money, getting pussy and the Dewey decimal system.

However, I'd be a remiss if I only pointed at the dark side of masculinity. Where there is the shadow of masculine, there is always the feminine to complement it. It is seen in the form when people refuse to own up to their own circumstances. There is always plenty of blame to go round the table. By refusing to take responsibility for our situation we essentially pass on the remote control of our lives to someone else.

You'd think the dark side of masculinity or femininity can be dangerous. Wait until you encounter the dark side of technology. For instance, how we discovered atomic energy only to make that into a bomb that has the potential to reduce entire cities to dust in the blink of an eye. Technology has also bred in us an excessive concern for the face value of our experiences. Sure, it has the potential to land us on Mars, but can also reduce the worth of a vacation to that one perfect selfie. We are becoming more and more concerned with making it appear that our lives are happening than making it actually so.

Then there is the concept of money that is, well, really not all that harmful so long as it is treated as a means to an end. It is really the rat-race concept that comes with it that keeps us from ever fully exploring the Self. It is the unhealthy attachment that is bred into us since school years of being in competition with the next guy rather than with ourselves. Always hunting for a future success and never being fully relaxed or satisfied with the present moment. Is it any wonder that the matrix breeds the rat race?

This chase binds us to the social collective design of reality whereby the individuality of a person is lost in the great sea of the herd mentality. Conformity is made ever more welcome in the matrix. On the other hand, a rebellious spirit expressing full individuality faces a crushing force on every turn. As such we are more inclined to trade in our individuality for the comfort of the matrix. We never figure out our true desires, to know where we truly belong. And before we know it, our courage runs out, life passes us by and we're left bitter, cold and faint-hearted, forever bound to satisfy the social norms. This is the price of conformity – everyone likes you, but you yourself.

When everyone receives the same programming from society and the culture, it is very difficult to keep one's authenticity and stay loyal to one's desires against the odds. No matter how enlightened you are, or how hard you try, the matrix is always conspiring to keep you in it. It consumes people just to spit out more non-programmable characters. As soon as you let your guard down, you'll find yourself slowly slipping back. If you gain a bit of perspective and self-awareness you will become more attuned to how circumstances are designed to take you away from yourself and your inner world, and land you in a desolate place of resistance and a distorted version of a higher reality. But, then again, the soul wouldn't have chosen the Earth experience if it wasn't for its unique challenges.

Now, the matrix in itself with its normal, everyday means is a Universe on its own. If you intend on creating a Universe within it that is besides the ways of the matrix, the matrix will retaliate and try to submerge your reality within its force. But, a bigger reality than the Earth matrix is the matrix of consciousness of the over-souls. Which matrix you are a part of is decided by the one you allow yourself to interact with the most. The constancy of the interaction in itself requires a level of self-mastery. Remember, however gruesome or ruthless the matrix may seem, it is only a reflection of your inner world. This is the key to breaking the matrix. Hell and heaven are pretty much the same hologram. It depends on the perspective that you look at it from.

Perspectivism has a great role in deciding your reality and the potential to turn any experience into gold. Two different people can go through the same experience and have two different takes on it which then decides their sense of being, of reality. Be it in the form of lessons or finding lost parts of ourselves - we can find treasure in the darkest corners of our experience.

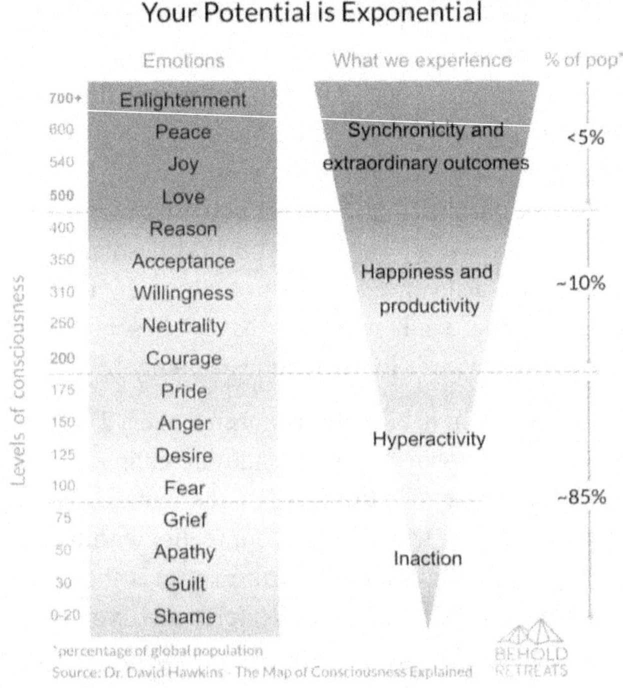

<u>Prompt: Embodying evermore lighter emotions and ascending</u>

In the Utopia, that is this world, there has to be no excessive pain than the pain of growth. You can always choose compassion and understanding rather than pain to move you forward, to accept change. The trauma and pain are just rejected parts of us. By the nature of the psyche, that seeks wholeness, the harder we reject parts of us, the greater momentum they'll gain in finding expression in the outer world. Until and unless integration happens, you continue to encounter your shadow everywhere outside of yourself. The shadow selves tend to play a decisive role in shaping the outer reality.

You, as a co-creator of your reality, are designed to formulate inner and/or outer experiences that cater to our specific vibration. The vibration in essence is the design of day-to-day living that imprints your consciousness in the web of the matrix consciousness. This is why when a person lifts up their consciousness they help the entire planet.

So, what should be your design? Think about it. What is your idea of happy, joyful and chill? Is it game night with friends or a relaxed afternoon with a good book? Is it emptying out your bank accounts and heading off on a forever vacation? Live a life with nothing but neon nights ahead and finding a cure for everything in the form of a pill. Before you stick to a design you must be aware of two concepts - suppression and overload.

Suppression is stillness to the point of no activity and overload is when you exhaust your nervous system through activity over a prolonged period of time. While the former is voluntary, the latter is vastly involuntary and is brought on by the use of drugs. Suppression is calming for the nervous system and the organs, and hence, good. But just like an unused car in a garage, inactivity for long periods of time can cause it to rot and loose its functionality, suppression can lead to atrophy. And atrophy is deadly. Similarly, overload can cause wear and tear in the organs.

Suppression and overload are applicable on emotions or the ego which has a counteractive effect on the nervous system and the organs. These are also the two gateways to a spiritual awakening. A tear in the ego is synonymous to a tear on the curtain separating the conscious and the unconscious.

In order to create calm and peace, it is important to collaborate with the soul. Otherwise, a person is likely to hit one of these two states. You'll find that things that lack soul lose their gleam pretty quickly. However, if you build something with a lot of heart the shine sustains on. Think about this when you think about what you want in life. Sometimes when a person feels a lack in a particular section of their life, they tend to gravitate towards creating things that fill these gaps. The point is not to stop there and just be satisfied with filling the lack. It is moving above and beyond the potential of the current best version of you.

Does this all mean that you become self-servient to the extreme? Well, you could be anything and have any formula for life so long as you're willing to detach from your personal story and give yourself a clean slate. Like Nietzsche would say it's the herd mentality and its mediocrity that one must strive to avoid.

A person, who is not well individualized, would rarely know what their design is. They are just shoved around in the world like backgammon pieces on a board. To use Heidegger's terminology, they become the "das-man", doing things solely because "that's what they do".

As important as self-awareness is, it is only the first step towards becoming the master of your own reality, of weaving a unique thread in the collective consciousness that corresponds to your signature vibe. And thus, your consciousness evolves, as you become more and more of yourself and less a part of the collective reality. Once you get over the baggage, the trauma and the suffering, you'll find the cosmic giggle getting back to you. This is because things mean only as much as you deem them to mean. This is the paradox of life and the key to begin reprogramming your reality.

But, however, will you control your outer reality when you have no control over yourself? There are several ways you can approach this question. The unconscious will continue to create experiences outside of ourselves to teach us lessons that are meant to be taught to harness the soul's potential and purpose. Fixing the inner via the outer is one way. Another way is to control the inner by bringing control to your thoughts and recognizing the inner voice via intuition. Intuition, being in sync with the universal heartbeat, is pertinent in the embodiment of your signature vibe.

Until and unless the body's intentions match the intentions of the mind, there will be no action. Inaction will breed stagnancy. In such tumultuous moments of life, you will find yourself inevitably reverting back to familiarity through the intentions that other people around you have set for you. The intentions that meet action manifest into physical reality. It's as simple as that. But, remember, it takes a truly courageous individual to face the glory, horror and shadows of their true being.

The grand design of the human being was always meant to be multi-dimensional. Hence, it is faulty to condense ourselves into a limited paradigm of straightforward thinking. It is giving too much attention to one form of consciousness that tips the scale and leads to the formation of the shadow. The shadow is the part of you that you ignore. There will be no tipping of scales, no formation of shadows, if there were a sort of a partnership between the material and the immaterial, conscious and unconscious, heart and mind, body and soul.

This requires acute awareness of not only one's physical being but also of the etheric and the unconscious. One of the ways to do this is through shadow work. Another way is to bring awareness into the things you engage yourself with, being mindful and present. Then there is talking to your body parts. Talking to your body parts and yourself is recognizing the consciousness everything holds. It helps us to recognize individual desires and stored trauma and eventually heal and attain alignment with the soul by healing the trauma and unifying these desires. The organs and everything in you form individual universes, hence, when you talk to your body parts, you take on the voice of God.

This is how one reaches multidimensionality and possibly gets to experience the bliss of soul embodiment. The downside of interconnectivity, meta-verse and technology is that we rarely pay much attention to the internal variables in deciding the value of our experience. Certainly, you risk being deemed psychotic if you choose to go at life via the inside out. But largely it is a matter of preference and the introversion or extraversion of an individual.

If you manage to establish a connection with your higher self through trust, fall and surrender, you get a hands-on lesson towards figuring out the specific algorithm of life. Or you could just hit four pipe smokes of DMT and get to experience the actual meta-verse. Either way, you'd be asked to get a hold of yourself and your reality.

If you take this journey of self-actualization, well, you'd be living the fulfilled version of yourself. The only thing that stands between one character and another is - you. Think of embodiment of your higher vibes as an investment to your character, the character that you're willing to play at life with.

Be cautioned against pushing your boundaries too fast, lest you shall risk your sanity. Dissociation from reality occurs when there is too much influx between the conscious and the unconscious. So be kind and gentle to yourself, always. Tell yourself good things and focus on your positives to have a solid, loving foundation for your character. Remember you have an eternity.

Mastery comes through practice. In order to speak the language of the Universe, you must understand unconditional love but love will not be gentle. The painful forms come in the form of lessons. Being human, we tend not to avert from learned behavior until we are knocked head over heels by the loving, benevolent hands of the Universe. The idea is to reduce the pain, to bring it to a place of integrity and acceptance.

Think of all the stories and lives you've known, everything in the Universe stems from a deep sense of love. To its minute essence, everything can be seeped down to a form of unconditional love. Sometimes the reasoning may be buried too deep for us to notice. It could take cruel, ugly and hellish forms. Or it could be utopian. You just have to have the courage to take a dive into the depths. Being detached from the stories and the drama that comes with human life can provide a sense of courage to explore our own inner depths which can then help in unleashing the creative power of the shadows.

With this realization we hit a sense of childlike-wonder. Think of yourself as a spoiled child to the Universe, you can have it all; you just have to ask and have the courage to face the consequences of your decision. You see, what you ask for can take many forms. So be specific in your mind towards the form of what you want. If you somehow manage to create something from your true essence – the bliss will continue on. Keep sorting yourself until you attain true sovereignty and freedom.

NOW IT'S ONLY YOU

λευκός have you been shedding your skin, your layers? Gone are fixed identities and definite options and opinions. Keep casting your shackles aside even if you fear that you are releasing too much. And then perhaps you shall cease to exist. You shall cease to exist only as long as you have known yourself to be thus far. Another emanation of you awaits. Something more beautiful and true. Yet here you are at the pruning stage like a gardener for the soul. Shall the garden spring to life or the denuding process be rather too much and unintentionally kill off the garden altogether, fear not, your soul is made of hearty stuff. It can handle a lot of culling and will shine brighter for it. Put your own tales aside, as dramatic as they may seem right now and prepare to be entranced by the greater story teller. The living poets of love as you are entranced in a tale of your unfolding divine destiny.

GROUND ZERO

Do not be so heavenly minded that you are no Earthly good.

Generally, the perception log of an individual is only accessible from the 'beginning' of this life – our birth, even though it may contain a log of past lives. However, in certain cases these perceptions seep through to affect the next life. Particularly in cases of violent deaths, the Perception log may not be properly sealed and a person may subconsciously experience 'leakages' from previous parts of the log.

The subconscious, which Jung termed as the unconscious, has no concept of time. Having no concept of time, it stores all the lifetimes and timelines that it has ever been in. Often, tragic deaths, unresolved complexes and relationships that are left unhealed are carried forward into the present. It may manifest as illnesses, trouble in interpersonal relationships, or interference in the normal flow of life.

Dolores Cannon, known as the pioneer of lost knowledge, developed the technique called Quantum Healing Hypnosis Therapy. Through somnambulistic hypnosis[1,] the brain is taken into a deeply relaxed state. During the theta brain state, the conscious mind is taken completely out of the picture. Dolores used this technique to tap into past lives where the perception log remained open.

She found that whilst the consciousness does inhabit the human body, it is by no means restricted to it. It takes many forms, such as rocks, rivers, trees, wind, oceans, sea creatures, dogs, and a myriad of other things. Pretty much everything has a form of consciousness. They even regressed back to lifetimes when they were on dimensions with rules completely different from what we know on Earth to be. They saw landscapes and realities that went beyond human comprehension.

There were many who regressed back to the Source, and gave pretty much the same description of it with minor fluctuations. Some saw it as an aurora borealis, shrouded in many colors. Others described it as a bright light like the Sun filled with warmth. In each of these descriptions there remained a constant, that the Source was filled with an overwhelming amount of unconditional love. And if you think about it, really, love is a rather warm feeling, isn't it?

Now if Source were light, then souls can be thought of as little motes of light that embody the Source. In other words, the Source can be thought of as unity consciousness and the souls as separate strands of this singular entity. The nature of consciousness is to move towards greater novelty and unity. Its function is creation, be it constructive or destructive.

Prompt: Souls leaving the Source

Now, think infinity. How can there be only a single Source of consciousness in an infinite Universe? If the Source is a higher state of consciousness then it is only your point of view that assigns them that value. There is always a Source above the Source. The purpose of lower consciousness is to ascend to higher and that of higher is to ascend to yet another higher state of consciousness. The soul of a person seen from the human perspective is the higher consciousness that seeks reintegration back into its original state.[2]

There can be several reasons why a soul disintegrates into various vessels. It can be for retrieval of another part of itself, it can be because the lower timelines seek correction, it can also be because the soul is too close to the light and the intense desire to stay with the light causes polarity leading to disintegration. The reasons are as numerous as there are stars in the sky.

When we are with the Source aka when we are whole, we have two options - either chill and hang for all of eternity, aka, to remain in eternal stagnation or to go out and create. Stagnancy might feel familiar and comfortable but in eternity, it is the one term that comes closest to describing hell. So, every once in a while, we must separate from the Source, from our soul, in order to create new worlds and make corrections should these new worlds start to malfunction.

Now, suppose you are chilling back with your soul family. A task, a correction, a mission, or simply an experience calls upon the soul. And thus, the soul sends a part of itself away into these timelines where it is needed the most. One of these timelines is you living your life on Earth. However, Earth is one of the trickiest places in the multiverse to be in.

Free will granted to humans is like a child handling heavy machinery. It is bound to breed chaos. But this is the truth of the Universe. Chaos breeds creation. Understanding the chaos of your world is bringing some sense of mastery to your existence. I understand that some feel Earth is a place of heavy emotions and energetic intentions which will leave a fragment wanting a bullet between its human head. But these intentions can only bother you as much as you allow yourself to align with these intentions. The heaviness makes creation and manifestation[3] slightly more difficult than in the lighter planes of existence. As such, only master manifestors are allowed access to the Earth plane. The soul is not accustomed to such heavy vibrations. As such, only a very small part of it is present in the human body at any given time. And sometimes even this small part is lost in the muck and mire of third dimensional existence. But fret not, a lost spirit can be found again by bringing a little self-awareness and lightness into your being.

Another kick-you-in-the-nuts rule of school Earth is that you are made to forget your connection to the miraculous, terrible beauty that is the over-soul. And all that is good, beautiful and life-saving is lost after being harvested into the matrix (reference next chapter).

The desire for self-awareness is met with revealing your soul to yourself – the good and the bad. Your capacity to hold this truth decides whether you are centered in awareness or distortion. When you dismantle your being you're left with the bare minimum that corresponds to your authentic self. Essentially, digging out your authentic self is undoing the programming that led to its burial. Remember, sometimes the authentic self can be a bit daunting and/or depressing. It depends on how farther away it has been taken away into the shadows. (refer Shadow Work)

With higher consciousness and light, we unleash multiple dimensions within the individual. However, Earth with its singular and linear concepts of caste, creed, time, and history breeds limiting and time-bounded intentions. This deprives us off the pleasure of reaching deep into our soul to find something true and long-lasting.

Earth is also a place of choices. As far as embodiment is concerned the choice boils down to several options, i.e., to be the matrix version of yourself that comes from conformity, to be the shadow version of yourself that comes from ignoring disowned versions of yourself, to be the light version of yourself with an excessive concern for goodness or to be whole that has the capacity to peacefully hold both dark and light.

An obsession for anything leads to a heavy polarity. A great desire towards something generates an aversion from something else. This calls attention towards practicing non-attachment. In other words, for every decision for something there is something else that you must let go of. Each choice comes with its own impediments. If you do make the wiser choice, i.e., you choose yourself, you converge towards awakening avatar level consciousness.

By overcoming a complex situation through your faculties, you unlock greater wisdom and a higher version of yourself. Your energetic intentions decide which path you choose. Understanding the inner thoughts and intentions means having greater control over the outer world.

Most people think that they are being led on by what they see, but really, they are being led on by what they believe. Thoughts determine our beliefs and act as impersonal energies that control us more often than we control them.

Your thoughts are not personal to you. They are just fleeting energies that have a hold on you until you have a hold on it. Our emotional state is affected by what we think, how we view ourselves and the world.

The authentic self is buried under everything that we have ever been told, that we have accepted to be true, without it sitting well with our inmost self, as well as under the outer experiences that we make our own. In harnessing our true potential, we must learn to control our thoughts. The thoughts, emotions, will and desires interact with each other. If we can bend our beliefs, we can change our core thoughts and through that we can reach our authentic self.

The authentic self is a completely fulfilled version of us. It takes pain as lessons, joy in its seasons and growth as it comes. There is no need and no rush to be at the endgame right this second, right this moment. This is not to say that there is no room for it. There is plenty of room and plenty of time to assess our emotions in case we reach an overload. But only once we have fully assessed and assimilated the trauma into understanding and acceptance, will we be back on track.

Love is the only word in the English dictionary capable of describing the synthesis between the inner and the outer world. The soul, being an eternal source of love, makes our life easier, if we come into alignment with it.

The cycle of life and lessons is infinite. Its beginning is the end and the end is the beginning. Whether the cycle starts in a lower or higher dimension depends upon the choices and events that have transpired in between and whether you have managed to shift your vibration. However, if you don't shift your vibration and learn your lessons, then bam! – Here comes the same cycle all. over. again. Like I said, there is no rush.

---

1. It is the third deepest level of hypnosis. The fourth and final stage includes coma.

2. If you are a child then your God is a man, and if you are a man then your God is a child. – C.G. Jung

3. Manifestation is the idea of bringing something you want into existence through action led aspirational-thought practices. "Desire without forethinking gains much but keeps nothing. But pleasure is power and therefore it moves." Forethinking united with pleasure succeeds.

MR. TRICKSTER, IS THAT YOU?

They put people on my back and made me go crazy. And then they tried to hide it from me. I hate them for that. The one thing that could've saved my sanity and kept me from going over the edge was the truth. And that was hidden from me because people don't see the world eye to eye. They are full of evil and malice, and so they think, the people around them hold evil intentions as well. I can't for the life of me figure out why things happened the way they did. I can't find any explanation for the loss of my sanity, no explanation for hearing the things that I did.

Blue rays attract negative auras into their field – to transmute it into something better.

I guess that's why this shitty reality didn't feel as bad as it was. I am bound by my nature to project hell into heaven.

I don't think I will ever be able to forgive them though – not for lifetimes. I don't even want to acknowledge the fact that they exist or that any of it is real. The hatred in me burns as bright as the morning sun. Heh. At least I rediscovered this side of me. I'm glad.

Perhaps it's hate that makes me say these things. When everything burns out in its light – I don't know how I would be left feeling. But for now, if there is a devil out there, I will gladly sell my soul. If you take selling your soul lightly then perhaps you don't understand its full implication. But then again I am blinded by rage.

Perhaps it was the devil all along and this was some great ruse to get me to concur and I will be back lifetimes after lifetimes to retrieve this part of me. But that's just what hell feels like. It feels like forever.

That doesn't sound quite right.

I can't stop mourning the loss of my innocence and my divinity.

It has to be a game. Since I was warned about it all those years back.

"Your life will feel like a movie." A half-hearted solace for all that happened?

Or maybe it was just me that overreacted. That's quite possible. But that doesn't explain so many things - like the voices, what they said and how they coincided with real circumstances. How could that have been had it all simply been a loss of sanity? What wall did I break? Perhaps it was the ego that broke - standing as a barrier between the inner and the outer - worlds. So all of the unconscious had to be made conscious. The consequences of me being too heavenly minded.

Maybe latent powers that were bound to wreak havoc or maybe I am still being too dreamy not knowing where I am.

I guess I can settle for all sorts of explanations now. My bandwidth has been broadened and my wiring has been messed with. Nothing is black and white anymore. Or rather everything is black and white at the same time. EVERYTHING IS GRAY!

Perhaps the devil dreams of heaven as well. And is driven mad with rage over not being able to find it in his long walks of eternity.

I thought when you strip back enough of your layers, you'll find your true self. But it's just emptiness waiting to be filled in. The choices we make in filling this emptiness is what reveals where we are in the spiritual path, I guess.

It's lonely out here. Is it better than being thrown into a herd where you follow every instinct that someone else chooses for you? I don't know. Free will is a scary concept. My mind is spiraling with indecision. What do I fill it with? What if I screw up? Anxiety gnaws away at the last bit of self-control. I feel scared.

Things are just things. I feel imprisoned by my own beliefs.

Do you remember how you were locked away by your own thoughts? Crying is disorienting.

Loneliness causes anxiety. People run to the crowd to sell their freedom. Is it worth it?

Freedom is dizzying but yet exciting.

Courage is an affirmative answer to the shocks of existence.

And to create requires courage.

ENTER THE VOID

Living in two realities at once is a scary existence.

A is for anger.

B is for broken.

C is for craving.

D is for deranged.

E is for eager.

F is for false hope.

G is for gore.

M is for monsters.

N is for your name.

O is for overcoming.

P is for poison which they swallow to awaken.

Q is for questioning.

R is for reminiscing.

S is for safety.

T is for tethered.

U is for unaffected.

V is for the vultures who feed off your fear.

W is for wondering.

X is the mark stamped on your head.

Y is for yelling.

Z is for zoned out.

Prompt: The Void is A Floating Mirror in Space

The void is like a floating mirror in space. If you stare into it, you'll find only a reflection staring back. In the fourth dimension of consciousness, light goes to lengths to assign void the meaning of love and darkness holds fear. But the void can take any form.

It can be cold and unendurable with no end at sight. This is hell. It is a state of limbo, of being caught in your errors, with no forward motion in sight. An eternal cycle of doom and damnation – it is torturous to keep repeating the same cycle over and over again. But it is only through hell that we come across the heroic stories of rising above oneself.

The shadow world is the void spaces in between your mind - imprisoned into this world of total darkness inspired by unawareness. And you are the jailer. These are the removed aspects of you that lacked nurture and care, imprisoned by the limiting beliefs that you harbor about yourself.

The void can also be a place of rest, rebirth, and awakening. It is where you face your shadows. For only once you've stayed long enough with yourself will you learn to recognize who you are and what you want. It is where you learn your shadows and give it the attention it demands. To make light of all of your shadow is to become whole.

What is the price of getting stuck in the void? It could be your sanity, your life, your identity. The void holds many fears. However, it is the great denier, the great untruth. It is that which is most unspoken about, but yet most thought about. There is no need to fear the void, for with its release there is again life which far exceeds that which we know.

In the void, everything is forgiven but not forgotten. However, those who would deny this life, we would caution by improper use, that is by suicide or of that nature; one generates an energy which follows you into the other side. And it is then necessary to be dealt with on the other side. It is, and never will be okay to cast off a living body before its time. It is a waste that is never to be tolerated.

Prompt: The beginning is the end and the end is a new beginning

"We are the hollow men

We are the stuffed men

Leaning together

Headpiece filled with straw. Alas!

Shape without form, shade without color,

Paralyzed force, gesture without motion."

-S. Eliot, The Hollow Men

Be careful not to build too many walls around you. Rest assured it is far better to be seen as vulnerable, than to be seen as something that you are not. People often create from pain, loneliness, hurt and in an attempt to keep on a happy façade, they refuse that any of it generates through them. This is the real danger of humanity. Every instance you have projected your shadow onto someone else is a chance missed to be whole. This will be used to cultivate belief systems that keep you tethered to a lower version of yourself. Every intention, from you or someone else, that was invested to create the person that you are will be at war against the version of you trying to break free.

The ones who refuse to own themselves will be at cross with those who don't. You will feel the true horror of the shadows when you have entered the void. Entry into the shadow world is just as difficult as coming out of it. But at the end of the tunnel there is the reward of finding your truest self. At every entrance back into the whole reality, is an intention that you have used to stay untrue to yourself, or suppress yourself. This is what happens when you attempt to regain control over your consciousness, consciously.

The real tragedy is forgetting who you are. It is when you are at the total mercy of someone else's shadow. To have your voice taken away from you is nothing short of a terrible accident. Remember, whatever you give out into the Universe has a way of finding itself back to you. So, if you abandon your shadow - and with it your whole self - it will not only abandon you but also grow hostile.

The faulty experience that the matrix offers is to be absorbed in someone else's story. When this happens, you are linking yourself with an energetic cord to them.

The reason for shadow work is that a whole ego realizes enlightenment quicker than a fragmented one. Once the shadow is dissolved into the ego, nothing exists to cast the shadow. The shadow is the dark side of the light chasers. It helps us understand that in the right circumstances anyone could just as easily be another Hitler. But just because your character possesses a lot of darkness that does not mean you must act it out.

Entering the void and assimilating the shadow simply gets you closer to self-mastery. To realize that we are no different from the worst people on this Earth destroys our sense of isolation. The only thing standing between you and them is you don't act out your worst intentions. It also helps you rise above the victim-perpetrator cycle and gain sovereignty over your being.

It is important to exercise your free will. If you do not, then, you risk having your story written by someone else, possibly, someone inferior to you. This is very much a possession, of being hijacked by someone else's will. Living in a reptilian world, this is not an uncommon occurrence. This is why, now more than ever, more people are being called to take charge of their situation, to take control of their divinity.

To have greater control on oneself is to have greater control on our timelines. Through following your intuitions, you can pick and choose from these timelines. The intuition is in sync with the universal heartbeat of the Universe. Ascension into a higher version of yourself can only happen when you embody evermore lighter emotions through detachment, which is, of course, easier said than done. In the end, you are only tethered to yourself and have to carry the consequences of your own decision. But being too precise or too deliberate in your actions can deprive you off the joy of life.

Love will save us all and love will not be easy. It's like the saying goes, don't do it for love, do it from love. The heart center, which is known to emanate at the frequency of love, has the ability to bring the unconscious will to body intelligence. It is one of the most important centers in the mind-body-spirit complex. Translated that means whatever you give care and attention to, in other words, whatever you focus yourself on manifests into the outer reality. However, this is only true for someone leading a heart centric life. Without the heart chakra acting as a filter between the lower and upper chakras, the energy shoots right up to the third eye chakra. This comes out as being overly analytical and logical about every situation.

When you are lost within the contents of your own mind, it is easy to twist any simple thing into an intellectual, conceptual framework that matches your own storyline. It is easy to get lost within the jungle of our own mind. This comes out as a rigidity of character that finds environments, anything outside of its comfort zone, as hostile and misses out on a lot of opportunities that could've been met otherwise. Denying shining the light of awareness onto the contents of your mind is depriving yourself of unconditional love.

Denying the light of awareness is most commonly met as a trauma response. There are parts of you that get suppressed when something occurs that surpasses the comprehension of the nervous system. This shock absorption fragments the consciousness into multiple parts that have to be then retrieved through shadow work.

Nature and humans have a flow, each having their highs and lows. However, those with a rigid obsession with logic can bind their fate with something unnatural, that goes against the flow of nature, and drag themselves into really heavy vibrations.

Since on Earth, pain and fear are some of the most deeply felt emotions, the heaviest intentions are inspired through them. It is its suppression or overload that initiates a person to a spiritual experience. The most traumatic experiences can be a point of no return from the hero's journey. Understanding past trauma is saving yourself from the virulent hands of fate.[1]

---

1. Fate and prophecy are interconnected. Prophecy is divine timing waiting for you to embody a certain version that can go on to fulfill a specific task.

FRAGMENTS

You will be blinded by the light.
You may just have to stand and fight.

For darkness is for the special few.
It's something hidden from your view.

Insidious feeling inside my being;
Crawling inside ripe for its freeing.

Look in my eyes between your screams;
Finally realize just what I mean.

I AM THE SHADOWS

"When consciousness is not present, suffering usually takes its place, and we are given the choice to become conscious by examining the relevancy of our experiences and the events that acted as catalysts to our new understandings, or to cycle in our suffering. Hence the ancient wisdom "pain is inevitable, suffering is optional.""

- Sarah Elkhaldy

I feel like I am caught in the ghosts of time. The forward movement paralyzes me with indecision. And looking back is no use. The past is gone and in dusts. I am in a perpetual state of letting go and I don't know how much I have lost.

It's difficult to keep up with consciousness. It's difficult to keep up with the truth. Maybe because within the current paradigm of my reality I just can't handle knowing so much.

Upon a long forgotten dream someone must have waged a war on my psyche. Maybe it was me.

But it's difficult to say where I end and they begin. Lol. I am scared shitless to ground within my own being, for I catch one of those shadows I done been created.

> - Or maybe I'll find the gold.

When you ignore them for long enough they become darker and denser.

Sometimes I just mentally give up on mission Earth, altogether, and that's a shameful thing to admit.

My mind is divided. There is nothing to keep the order that is bred out of this chaos.

I feel like a divided mind and body is what has manifested this chaos in the first place. The circle of life, huh?

A shameful retort that would floor me for days.

The feeling of being only half of what I am is no good.

SHADOW WORK

"How do you find your shadow?"

"How do you find the dragon that has swallowed you?"

- C.G. Jung

The amount of reality you can hold at any point is the amount of truth you can hold about yourself without wanting to run backwards. Enter – the shadow.

The shadow is the mirror image of ourselves that we cannot see. The wholeness of a person is both the light and dark parts of them. To deny darkness is to deny half of oneself. We must recognize that we are both capable of good and evil. To avoid conflict, we deny emotions within us which form the unconscious shadows.

The shadow is often seen as evil, dark and something to be avoided. However, the shadow is not something detached from oneself. It cannot and should not be avoided, for we will be going against ourselves. It has a compensatory role that seeks to restore our wholeness. For instance, the shadow of a criminal would have qualities like sincerity, relatedness, tenderness, etc. The shadow of a shy person would be commitment, responsibility, assertiveness, etc.

The shadow is not our enemy, but our friend. It has pure gold waiting to be integrated into our personality. The shadow only becomes hostile when it is ignored or misunderstood, that is when it takes control of us, because we are not willing to. We can either be led and guided in life by our shadow, or be dragged through life by it. It is the union of both good and evil that gives way to the transcendent. The shadows, if ignored for long enough, accumulate more energy than our ego until it erupts in overpowering rage.

Culture, acting as a great leveling factor, brings everyone down to the same level. We are all born whole. But culture demands that we live out only parts of ourselves. We divide the self into the ego and the shadow.

"Curiously, people resist the noble aspects of their shadow more strenuously than they hide the dark sides. To draw the skeleton out of the closet is relatively easy, but to own the gold in the shadow is terrifying. It is more disrupting to find that you have a profound nobility of character than to find out you are a bum." (Robert A. Johnson, Owning Your Own Shadow)

Shadow integration is gaining consciousness of good and evil. Robert uses the image of the seesaw to illustrate our personality. On the one side we have the acceptable qualities, and on the other side, there are the forbidden sides - the unacceptable qualities. No qualities can be discarded. It can only be moved between these two sides. A law prevails that a balance must be maintained in order to be in psychic equilibrium. The instability between these two sides is what causes mood swings. And if the seesaw is too heavily loaded, it may break at the center point. This is a psychosis. The psychosis is only cured when the conscious and unconscious are integrated into the self.

While we may want to hide the dark side from society, we must never hide it from ourselves. Robert writes, "To act is to sin. To create is to destroy at the same moment. We cannot make light without a corresponding darkness." We would love to have creativity without destruction but that is not possible. No one can escape the dark side of life. But we can pay the dark side intelligently so that the balance of light and dark is ultimately possible - and bearable.

The ego and the shadow come from the same source and exactly balance each other. The ego and the shadow together make whole. It is not perfection we must strive for but wholeness. This is how the joy of life is created - embracing our own humanity with its strengths and flaws, and not a one-sided goodness that has no vitality to life.

One has to honor one's shadow, for it is an integral part of oneself. But one must not push it onto someone else. Projection is easier than assimilation. The shadow will claim its dues in some form - intelligent or stupid. To refuse the dark side of one's nature is to store up or accumulate the darkness. This is later expressed as a black mood, or unconsciously inspired accidents.

The tendency to see one's shadow out there in a specific group of people is the most dangerous aspect of human society. It is only by taking one's shadow back in oneself can we return back to ourselves. It is common for two people's shadow to be on each other. To be in the presence of another's shadow and not reply is nothing short of genius.

Goethe's Faust is a great example in literature of the meeting of the ego and the shadow. Faust is a scholar who finds life meaningless and contemplates suicide. His seesaw has reached the breaking point. At this point he meets with his shadow - Mephistopheles. Through their perseverance Faust is saved from lifelessness and becomes capable of passion and Mephistopheles discovers his capacity to love. Love is the one word adequate to describe the synthesis of the ego and the shadow.

"People are as frightened of their capacity for nobility as of their darkest sides. If you find the gold in someone, he will resist it to the last ounce of strength. This is why we indulge in hero-worship so often." (Robert A. Johnson, Owning Our Own Shadow) All our energy lies in our shadow and ignoring it makes us feel lifeless. Facing our shadow fills us up with stamina which we can then use in our daily task.

The unconscious is ten times more powerful than the conscious. When one becomes tired of involuntary trips between the see-saw, a middle ground is sought. The middle-ground is not the great compromise that we fear but a place of ecstasy and joy. If we learn how to take the energy of the shadow and use it correctly, we set the stage for a whole new stage of life. One must give expression to the shadow in some way that it does not damage the lighter side.

The paradox of life is that treasure is to be found in the darkest corners. We will go to most painful paradox to confine ourselves to the useless experience of contradiction. Contradiction is barren and destructive and yet paradox is creative. Every human experience can be expressed in terms of paradox. Day has relevance only in contrast to night. Masculine has relevance only in contrast to feminine. Where would I be without you? Where would joy be without sobriety? These are not opposites, but necessities for human conditions.

So, what would we do with this paradoxical question that is at the base of every psychological problem? If we go at the question wrongly, we would go into a neurotic paralysis where we cannot act or be still. This is where suffering is intense.

"I can't be bothered. I can't be bothered to ride, the motion is too violent; I can't be bothered to walk, it's strenuous; I can't be bothered to lie down, for either I'd have to stay lying down and that I can't be bothered with, or I'd have to get up again, and I can't be bothered with that either. In short: I can't be bothered." (Soren Kierkegaard, Either/Or)

Paradox is the solution to despair. To think that one way of action is profane and another is sacred is to make a terrible misuse of language. This is the seat of most of the neurotic suffering in human kind. Belief restores and reconciles the opposition that has been torturing each of us. It helps us move from contradiction to the realm of paradox where we are able to entertain two contradicting notions and give them equal dignity.

The English poet William Blake also spoke about the need to reconcile both the light and the dark parts of ourselves. He said that we should go to heaven for form and hell for energy - and marry the two. Most people spend their entire life energy supporting the war of opposites between themselves. This only brings despair. In the miracle of paradox, it is good to win, it is good to lose. It is good to have; it is also not good to have. Each represents a reality, a truth. To stay loyal to paradox is to earn the right to wholeness.

Fanaticism is always a sign that one has adopted one of a pair of opposites at the expense of the other. The high energy of fanaticism is to keep one half of the truth at bay while the other half takes control. This always yields a brittle personality that is always right. But what has paradox to do with the shadow? It has everything to do with the shadow, for there can be no paradox - that sublime place of reconciliation - until one has owned one's place of shadow

and drawn it up to a place of dignity and worth. Conflict -
paradox – revelation: this is the divine progression.

The intersection of the divine and the human is the guide out
of the realm of conflict and duality. When one is tired or
discouraged by life that one can no longer bear to live, the
Self shows what one may do when the most herculean efforts
and the finest discipline no longer keeps the painful
contradiction of life at bay. Our own healing proceeds from
that overlap of what we call good and evil, light and dark.
The place where light and dark begin to touch is where we
have the most profound experience. We like to think that a
story is based on the triumph of good over evil; but the truth
is that good and evil are superseded and the two become one.

GO IT ALONE

With the strength of the heart and the integrity of the mind we can overcome anything.

It's sad and enlightening at the same time that I have to dissociate from my mind and turn to other people to find safety. After all the search I have found only one thing - the world can't give me anything that I can't give to myself.

Don't go too deep in the dark without a compass pointing out. You might get lost. But if you do and find yourself all alone, or worse, surrounded by unwelcoming shadows in the closet then simply take care of your physical body. The shadows might try to break your mind but remember you will never be served more than you can swallow. The spirit, body and mind will be taken care of if you simply align your physical activities with the spirit. Also, remember to take it slow. Slow down your pace, slow down your activities. Don't be in a rush to know too much too fast. You will give yourself an overload. There's plenty of time to fill your little head with all sorts of magical things. Acknowledge the shadows in the closet lest they shall haunt you or worse, they will try to control you for the rest of your life. Don't be too rational when you meet them. Remember it is the rejected version of you so it is going to be difficult to acknowledge, difficult to bear. So be brave and shed the lights on your own truth. Do not try to escape your being when it becomes too much to bear. You are only delaying what needs to be made whole.

It's like they say, the truth will set you free, but first it will piss you off. Try not to interact with other people's shadows even when it seems unfair. It only fuels it and you risk getting caught in their trauma. The shadow loves attention and it will try to take you over if you get too involved. So, be careful, be strong in the mind and heart.

The world outside of you has an intelligence of its own. That what you try to run from will find its way back to you. Learn to live fearlessly, in the light but especially in the darkness, for it is the one that will serve you the most. You are wholly responsible for yourself. If you try to disown this responsibility in any way, it will become a burden. And just because you bow to no one, it doesn't mean you can't trust them. The world is a good, beautiful place. So, practice freedom and dependence in moderation. For the excess of anything is poison.

FINDING A TEMPLATE FOR LIFE AND LOSING TO DESPAIR

"The greatest of lessons come to us through madness, when it is sent to us as a gift of Gods."

- Socrates

<u>GRANDLY GESTICULATING IN THE PRISON OF MY OWN MAKING</u>

Why is everyone a jerk? Why am I alone? Do I not have a life? Am I depressed? Am I intelligent? Am I smart? Am I a genius? A loner. Where is my ego? Is this my ego? Why did I choose this? IDK. There is nothing to show for in real life, is there? Why are they obsessed with me? Why am I obsessed with myself? Why am I afraid to show it? Am I dangerous? I'm sad. Druggie? No. I'm different because I know more about myself than anyone knows of themselves. Or maybe that's just what I think. Why did I have to know so much? Was that my ego? So much sadness. So much hurt. Not enough juice left to rise above myself. Not enough courage. My powers are useless. My body is low. She cries when there's nothing to be upset about. What's left of life? What's left of life? I can't think of anything worthwhile. There's no one. Drugs? No. Maybe family and friends. There is nothing left. Everything has turned to shit. No one on Earth seems worth me. Nothing is worth it to me. They're all mindless clones, preoccupied with mundane things. How do I become a mindless clone? Do I want to be a mindless clone? Perhaps because I expect there will be no pain. And for pain – I don't want any of it.

"Life is not a problem to be solved. But a reality to be experienced."

Existence is a colossal risk; we can never know whether the way we choose to live is the right way. Anyone who fully realizes this is bound to feel angst. We thus come to know the nothingness of existence, the utter uncertainty and illusion.

Kierkergaard's notion of trying to define a self is one of his many ironies, likely intended to produce despair in one who can figure out himself alone.

Finitude despair - Also called depressive psychosis. There is not enough freedom for the inner self. The individual lives any alternate way of life and cannot release himself from the trivial obligations that give him no value. By surrendering himself and others and holding on to people that have enslaved him in a network of crushing obligations. He chooses slavery because it is safe and meaningful but soon this too loses meaning. One has then died to life but must remain physically in this world, thus, the torture of depressive psychosis – to remain steep in one's failures and to justify it to continue to draw a sense of self-worth.

"The biggest danger, that of losing oneself, can pass off in the world as quietly as if it were nothing, every other loss, an arm, a leg, five dollars, a wife, etc. is bound to be noticed."

Infinitude despair - We have an infinite number of possibilities, and when we have to choose one, we become overwhelmed at the sheer amount of them. If you ask someone if they are an individual, they will undoubtedly say yes. However, one may possess the ability to freely act, but if one never uses it and gets lost in the infinite, thinking about an endless sea of possibilities, they are effectively not capable of freely acting. The infinitized person lacks a grounded self.

"While one sort of despair plunges wildly into the infinite and loses itself, a second sort permits itself as if it were to be defrauded by "the others". By seeing the multitude of men about it, by getting engaged in all sorts of worldly affairs, by becoming wise about how things go in the world, such a man forgets himself does not dare to believe in himself, finds it too venturesome a thing to be himself, far easier and safer to be like the others, to become an imitation, a number, a cipher in the world."

- Soren Kierkegaard, The Sickness Unto Death

One can try making sense of life by laying a worldview or template on it, but Kierkegaard would guarantee you that the template would eventually shatter and break. So, what do you do? Keep trying to make new templates and see if one works for you? Or maybe the template's the problem? Kierkegaard would tell you to start with yourself.

He believed that one must either live an aesthetic life which maximizes pleasure and kills boredom, or they can live an ethical life. But can one strike a balance between the two, by making the social life the ethical one and the personal life the aesthetic one? Or would that be too much on the psyche? Can one be a part of the world and yet remain oblivious to all that goes on in the world? Or would one lose oneself under the crushing obligations of the social norms? I believe that a balance is possible.

In the aesthetic life (inner life) one is ruled by passions and in the ethical life one is ruled by societal regulations (the outer world). Kierkegaard classified a third life which is the religious/spiritual one. I believe it can be used as a go-between the inner and the outer and keep them in a perfect balance.

AN EGOLESS WORLD: A MODEL TO UTOPIA OR DYSTOPIA?

The ego is like a curse for people here. One must have ego to move forward; without ego there would be no forward movement.

- Dolores Cannon, Convoluted Universe Part

Ego is the tool that defends the belief that we are all "separate" entities. By characterizing our experiences into "acceptable" and "unacceptable" we not only take away the wholeness of our experience, but also fuel the shadow's hostility. Ego can never die - it can only be made conscious so that it is no longer running the show.

Psychedelics may provide a temporary transcendence in the most mind-bending, awakening, awe-inspiring, peaceful, and unconditionally loving experience you could ever have. It's like returning back to your true nature.

However, while the experience of ego death is indescribably beautiful, it can also be indescribably horrific for those who are not aware of the spiritual path, and for those who resist the actual experience. Shamanic plants such as ayahuasca, DMT, and psilocybin mushrooms are powerful gateways to the Divine experience. One of the earliest documented bad trips was reported by Albert Hofmann, the chemist who discovered LSD. He started experiencing a bad trip and, in an attempt to soothe himself, requested some milk from his next-door neighbor who appeared to have become "a malevolent, insidious witch."

The ego creates intense defense mechanisms to try and hold on to a sense of control and power. However, as Terence McKenna once said, the abyss must be approached with courage, because only then can you discover that the fear is an illusion:

"Nature loves courage. You make the commitment and nature will respond to that commitment by removing impossible obstacles. Dream the impossible dream and the world will not grind you under, it will lift you up. This is the trick. This is what all these teachers and philosophers who really counted, who really touched the alchemical gold, this is what they understood. This is the shamanic dance in the waterfall. This is how magic is done. By hurling yourself into the abyss and discovering it's a feather bed."

The ego death, whether induced by psychedelics, existential crisis, or any traumatic situation takes away the Big I Am. When we are born we are given a Personality to fulfill our destiny. The ego, on the other hand, might add a feeling of uniqueness, [which may well be right], but we can also start to feel separate, our uniqueness gives us the false impression that we are better than other people, important, maybe far more important than anyone else - AND THIS IS EGO AND IT IS DEEPLY DESTRUCTIVE. We are not special; we are just simply different. And we have each been made different because we have a job to do.

The stronger the sense of 'I' - a very strong 'ego', the more separate we are and thus the more selfish and destructive we are too, because we feel no sense of unity with our fellow beings - humans, animals or the planet as a whole - at all.

A strong ego is deeply, deeply destructive.

And we are seeing the effect of this sense of separateness now. Everyone is telling other people what to do to save the planet, forgetting that they themselves are a part of it.

So a massive ego is doubly dangerous. It creates a false sense of importance so great that we can destroy the planet because of it. And the ego totally - and I mean totally - blocks out any spiritual input, thus the help we might receive to save us is denied.

THE HERO'S JOURNEY

The world is gold and in visions, when the vision ends we cannot bear to see the world. But the golden world is there all the time. It is a state of consciousness. It is an experience open to anyone, at any time. The kingdom of God is within. For the exploration of this inner world, one must go beyond the ego, and delve into the shadow.

To be in a situation where there is no way out, or to be in a conflict where there is no solution is the classical beginning of individuation or self-realization. In this state, the unconscious wants the hopeless conflict to end, in order to put ego-consciousness up against the wall so that one has to realize that whatever one does is wrong. This is an act of humility, that invites one to see beyond the ego to see that which is greater within ourselves.

It tells the story of a person encountering difficult life problems and their journey resolving it through personal transformation.

The hero's journey provides a template for all changes, intentional or unintentional. It is a re-conceptualizing of disorder into a hero's quest, rather than an external stressful task, shifting their attitude from active to passive, supporting them to become the "author of their own lives."

A central hero figure in Greek mythology is Achilles, the greatest of all Greek warriors. As a boy, he was guided by the wise centaur Chiron, tutor of gods and heroes, who instructed him in the arts of medicine, music, riding and hunting.

"..the essential function of the heroic myth is the development of the individual's ego-consciousness – his awareness of his own strengths for the arduous tasks with which life confronts him."

- Joseph L. Hendersen, Man and His Symbols

The significant life problem is a situation where the hero's existing knowledge and skills are no longer efficacious. In finding a solution, the Hero is required to leave his familiar, known world, and venture into the unknown. Significant life problems force us to change. However, most of us are reluctant to do so. Ignoring these matters forms unconscious snags which give us a state of impoverishment in our personality and inhibit the growth of the good qualities that lie dormant in our psyche, making our shadow blacker and denser.

"Fate leads the willing, and drags along the reluctant."

- Seneca, Letters from a Stoic, CVII

In the Hero with a Thousand Faces, Campbell identified that a Hero's Journey occurs in three sequential phases: separation, initiation and the return. However, we will be using the more modern and popular adaptation of Christopher Vogler, detailed in his work "The Writer's Journey", which is inspired by Campbell.

He proposes a 12 stage hero's journey.

1. The Ordinary World refers to one's familiar life: daily routine, the stresses and joys of work, family and social connections. A growing awareness is that something is not quite right. Life is somehow lacking.

2. The Call to Adventure: This is the second stage, which disrupts the comfort of the Hero's Ordinary World and presents him with a quest that must be undertaken. The Call to Adventure separates the person from the aspects of their previous life and causes anxiety. Many are overwhelmed and believe that their problem is beyond their capabilities leading to a third stage.

3. Refusal – This is a very common and important stage that communicates the risks involved in the Journey ahead. However, remaining in the refusal stage will lead to a deterioration in one's life and relationships. One finds himself with little or no motivation. At this crucial turning point, the hero desperately needs guidance leading to the fourth stage.

4. Meeting the Mentor – The mentor is the archetype of the wise old man. It is his role to assist the Hero's progress to the realization that personal change is a necessity for the resolution of his problem, giving him practical training, wise advice or self-confidence in order to overcome the initial fears, allowing him to move from inaction to action. These tutelary figures do not have to be a personal one. It can be a public figure, or anyone that you look up to as your ideal self. When the Hero is committed to change he enters the second phase of the Heroes' journey.

5. Initiation and Crossing the First Threshold – The hero now leaves the safe haven of the "Ordinary World" and enters the "Special World", an unfamiliar place, with his "dragon", his worst fear,

event, person, situation or memory long avoided. As trials become more difficult, the Hero hones his skills and gains experience. However, as the trials increase in complexity, the demands placed on the Hero lead to higher levels of anxiety, and his first confrontation with the dragon is likely to fail. Without help, he may consider giving up.

6. Tests, Allies, and Enemies – The Hero explores the Special World and encounters tests and enemies. Here he must seek Allies, friendly forces who support change attempts and decrease the Hero's isolation. A common barrier here is the fear of asking for help, for being seen as less than capable or for possibly being rejected. Ironically, vulnerability becomes a key skill in resiliency, rather than a sign of weakness.

7. Approach to the Innermost Cave – Here, one must make his final preparations before descending into the unknown. When the Hero is ready he faces the eighth stage.

8. The Supreme Ordeal – It is the greatest challenge yet, the moment when all looks lost for the Hero, many feel like they are "back at square one". Fortunately, Allies have witnessed this major setback and are present to assist the Hero. Over a period of time, the repeated confrontation with the dragon leads to the realization that what was once believed to be impossible is now possible. After facing the unknown and defeating the dragon, the Hero experiences a psychological death and rebirth. The death of an old aspect of one's self and the birth

of a new and more capable self. The Hero gains insights receiving this as his Reward (the ninth stage).

9. The Return – The journey is not over yet and now begins the tenth stage. The hero must hold his reward and make his way to the ordinary world, but on the way he is confronted with more enemies and dragons. However, the Hero knows that there's no way back and is motivated to keep going.

10. The Resurrection – The weary hero must experience a second psychological death, experiencing a resurrection with the attributes of his ordinary self in addition to the new insights from the journey and characters he has met along the road of life. He moves from dependence to responsibility. From silence, to finding his voice. The Hero has increased resilience and has learned how to regulate fear, sadness and other emotions that arise when taking action. He is now purified from the land of the dead and can now return home, leading to the twelfth and final stage.

11. Return with the Elixir – The elixir is the final reward earned in the hero's Journey. It is something for the Hero to share with others, or something with the power to heal: wisdom, love or simply the experience of surviving the special world.

The hero comes back to the Ordinary world with a new self, having faced the terrible dangers and possibly death, but now looks forward to the start of a new life.

This is not a one-time linear path, but a lifelong cyclical process.

"The quest to find the inward thing that you basically are."

- Joseph Campbell, The Power of Myth

One of Campbell's repeated phrases is to "follow your bliss."

"If you do follow your bliss you put yourself on a kind of track that has been there all the while, waiting for you, and the life you ought to be living is the one you are living. When you can see that, you can begin to meet people who are in your field of bliss, and they open doors to you. I say, follow your bliss and don't be afraid , and doors will open where you didn't know they were going to be."

DEATH

The devil with the dreams of heaven. A black angel of night. Light showered from the porcelain angels. You are the sword. Whoever attempts to wield you shall have to face their darkest nightmares.

It is only once we wake from death do we realize that it was all just a really profound dream, anyway. But we're gonna forget it, anyway.

Or perhaps they will be left with a bittersweet feeling that will cling on for long enough to make them wanna go back.

Make of that what you will.

The endlessness of the present moment stays. The feeling can be sublime and eternal. Or it can be, well, whatever you like !

CATALOGUE

---

https://www.thesap.org.uk/articles-on-jungian-psychology-2/carl-gustav-jung/jungs-model-psyche/#:~:text=Jung%20maintained%20that%20the%20pc he,as%20he%20called%20it%2C%20individuation.

allaboutheaven.org

The Red Book by C.G. Jung

Memories, Dreams and Reflections by C.G. Jung

Between Death and Life by Dolores Cannon

The Convoluted Universe 1,2,3 by Dolores Cannon